Hanna-Barbera's

THE GREATEST ADVENTURE
STORIES FROM THE BIBLE

THE NATIVITY

Based on a teleplay
by Dennis Marks

Story adaptation by
Bruce D. Johnson and Harvey Bullock

ABINGDON PRESS
Nashville

The Greatest Adventure

Derek and Margo are digging in the desert for things from the past. Their friend Moki, who lives nearby, is helping them.

One hot day the three friends are working when, suddenly, they begin to sink into the sand. "Quick-sand!" yells Moki. They tumble through space.

When they land, Margo, Derek, and Moki look around in amazement. They are in a huge room filled

with treasures from long ago. On a door at the end of
the room they find a mysterious message:

*All who enter these doors
go back in time.*

Margo touches the doors. Suddenly they swing open
and a bright light fills the room.

"Let's go!" says Margo.

One after another they step through the doorway
into the light...

THE NATIVITY

Joseph was a carpenter who lived in the town of Nazareth. One day he was making a table outside his house. Suddenly he heard trumpets. Roman soldiers in chariots thundered into the town square.

The captain stepped out. Everyone gathered around to hear what he had to say.

"Emperor Caesar Augustus says you must all pay more taxes," he said.

"More taxes!" the people whispered.

"Quiet!" shouted the captain. "You must pay the tax in the city where you were born. Pack up and go!"

Joseph went inside to talk to Mary, his wife. She was going to have a baby very soon.

"My family is from Bethlehem," he said.

"That means you and I—and the baby—have a long trip ahead of us," she said quietly. Then she smiled. "God will be with us. Remember the angel who spoke to me?"

"Yes," answered Joseph. "The angel Gabriel said you will have a son. His name will be Jesus. He will be the Son of God."

"To Bethlehem?" asked Mary.

"To Bethlehem," said Joseph.

Derek, Margo, and Moki rubbed their eyes and looked around. All they saw were sand and hills.

"Where are we?" asked Derek.

"In the desert," answered Margo. "I think we're in the Holy Land."

The three started off. They walked and walked, up one hill and down another.

"It's so hot," said Derek, stopping to wipe his face.

"I'm thirsty," said Moki.

Suddenly Margo shouted. "Look! An oasis!"

In the distance they saw a well surrounded by palm trees, tents, and camels. Travelers stopped there to rest and get water.

At the well Margo, Derek, and Moki met Yasha, a young shepherd. He was drinking from a goatskin.

"Would you like some water?" he asked Margo. He held up the bag and let a stream of water shoot into Margo's open mouth.

"Mmm," she gulped.

"Everybody's traveling home. For me, that's Jerusalem," said Yasha. "Would you like a ride?"

"Gee, thanks," said Derek, looking at the camel waiting nearby.

Yasha and his three new friends weren't the only ones on the road to Jerusalem. Three wise men from the East were following a bright star across the desert. They were looking for the place where the new king was to be born.

"Look how the star moves," said the first wise man.

"We must keep going," said the second. "Jerusalem is just ahead."

"Oh, the holy city. It's a perfect place for the birth of a king," said the third.

The wise men rode on, one behind the other.

The next day Mary and Joseph, along with many other travelers, stopped at the oasis. They were tired from their long journey. Mary knew the baby would be born soon.

"Let's rest here," said Joseph. "We'll be in Bethlehem by tomorrow evening."

Yasha led Derek, Margo, and Moki through the city gates into Jerusalem. They came to a busy marketplace. Merchants were selling foods Margo and Derek had never seen before. Other merchants were selling brightly colored cloth and beautiful pottery.

Just then Yasha and his three friends saw a crowd of people. In the middle stood the three wise men. They had followed the star to Jerusalem and were looking for the new king.

"Is there a new king in Jerusalem?" the first wise man asked.

Eli, King Herod's high priest, stepped forward and answered, "There is only one king here—Herod."

"But the star? We were sure the new king would be born here," said the second wise man.

"No, you must be mistaken," said Eli.

Disappointed, they turned away. Eli hurried off to tell Herod about the three strangers.

When Eli arrived at the palace, King Herod was sitting in his throne room.

"Sire, three men, dressed in rich clothes and jewels, have come to Jerusalem. They are looking for a new king called the Messiah."

"A new king?" shouted Herod. "I am Herod the Great, named by the Emperor himself. What makes anyone think there is a new king?"

Then Herod gave an evil smile. He had a plan. "Eli," he ordered, "bring the wise men to me. I'll send them to Bethlehem."

The three wise men went to see Herod. "I understand you are looking for a new king," said Herod. "As I remember, this new king will be born in Bethlehem, not Jerusalem. You'll have to go there to find him."

When the wise men had left, Herod called Eli. "Have some soldiers follow them. I want to know if the wise men find this new king."

Moki, meanwhile, had stayed in the marketplace. He was helping a fruit seller load melons onto a cart. Moki piled the melons too high. Suddenly, the cart broke. Melons rolled everywhere! Derek and Margo arrived just in time to rescue him. They ran off with the angry fruit seller close behind.

Hiding in an alley, they heard Eli say to Quintus, the soldier, "Follow the wise men to Bethlehem."

Derek and Margo looked at each other. "Three wise men? Bethlehem?" asked Derek.

"Yasha will take us. Let's go!" said Margo.

Mary and Joseph continued their long journey toward Bethlehem. Mary rode the donkey and Joseph walked along beside her.

Just as the sun was setting, Joseph pointed to a small village. "Mary, there's Bethlehem!"

"I think we'd better hurry," said Mary quietly.

"Come on, fella, we're almost there," said Joseph, patting the donkey.

They walked down the narrow streets looking for a place to stay. Finally, they came to an inn. The innkeeper was outside talking to some travelers. "No! No! No!" he exclaimed. "There are no rooms in all of Bethlehem. Everyone has come to pay his taxes."

As he turned to go inside, the innkeeper saw Mary and Joseph. "Please," he said, "don't ask me for a room. There just isn't one."

"It doesn't have to be a room," said Joseph, "just a place for my wife to lie down."

The innkeeper looked at Mary. "I have a stable. It's not even that. It's a cave for the animals."

"Thank you," said Joseph. "We'll take it."

The stable was dry and warm. Mary lay down on the soft hay. Some lambs, a cow, and the donkey stood quietly nearby.

Later that evening the innkeeper came to the stable. "I brought some blankets in case the baby is born tonight," he said.

Joseph stayed close to Mary. "Tonight will be a very special night," she said smiling.

Not far from Bethlehem the three wise men stopped to rest. They sat talking by their campfire. Each one had a small chest in front of him.

The first one opened his chest. It was filled with gold. "This is the gift I bring to the new king."

The second one opened his chest and breathed deeply. "I'm bringing him frankincense."

"I'm bringing him myrrh," said the third, opening his chest.

"I had a strange dream," said the second wise man. "King Herod cannot be trusted. I don't think we should tell him about the new king."

The other wise men agreed. They would not return to Jerusalem.

Derek, Margo, and Moki walked along under the night sky. Yasha rode the camel. They were not far from Bethlehem when Derek pointed to the sky. "Look!" he cried.

Margo gasped. "It's the Star of Bethlehem! We were right!"

Suddenly a bright light shone down on some shepherds watching their sheep in the hills nearby. The shepherds covered their eyes and knelt down. They were afraid.

But an angel appeared and said, "Fear not, for I bring good tidings of great joy. Unto you is born this day in the City of David, a Savior, who is Christ the Lord. You shall find the Babe wrapped in swaddling clothes and lying in a manger."

Just then Derek saw the Roman soldiers riding off toward Jerusalem. "Oh, no!" he cried. "The soldiers will tell Herod about the new king. The baby will be in danger. We've got to stop them!"

"Derek, let them go," said Margo quietly. "Don't you remember? An angel will warn Joseph. He and Mary will take the baby to Egypt where he'll be safe."

The three friends followed the star to Bethlehem. They stopped a short distance from the stable. In the manger, Mary held the baby Jesus.

Moki's eyes opened wide. "Mary? Joseph? The star! You mean tonight . . ."

"Yes, Moki. This is Christmas," said Margo softly.

"Look," whispered Moki, "there are the wise men with their gifts."

Suddenly the sky over Bethlehem was filled with angels and bright light. The angel said, "Glory to God in the Highest, and on earth, peace, and good will toward men."